CALUM KERR is a writer, editor, Teaching Fellow in Creative Writing at the University of Southampton's Winchester School of Art, and Director of the UK's National Flash Fiction Day. His work has appeared in a number of places—online and in print—and was featured on BBC Radio 4's *iPM* programme. He live in Southampton with his wife, his stepson, two cats and a dog.

Other books by Calum Kerr

FLASH-FICTION COLLECTIONS

31
Braking Distance
Lost Property

NOVELS

Undead at Heart

TEXT BOOKS

York Notes Advanced: The Kite Runner
York Notes AS & A2: The Kite Runner

Apocalypse

a flash-fiction novella

2014 flash365: volume 1

Calum Kerr

Published by Gumbo Press

First Published 2014 by Gumbo Press.
Printed via CreateSpace.

Gumbo Press
18 Caxton Avenue
Bitterne
Southampton
SO19 5LJ
www.gumbopress.co.uk

All work ©2014 Calum Kerr

The moral right of the author has been asserted

All rights reserved. No part of this publication may be
reproduced, stored in a retrieval system,
or transmitted, in any form or by any means,
electronic, mechanical, photocopying, recording or
otherwise, without the prior permission of the
publishers.

A CIP Catalogue record for this book
is available from the British Library

ISBN 978-1495351587

Contents

Party Time	9
Stalking	12
Dude	14
The Third Time's the Charm	17
Uluru	21
Grab the Wheel	23
The After Party	26
Shock and Awe	29
Roadside	31
They Rise	34
Eternal Love	36
P. O. V.	39
The Hangover	40
Writing The End	43
Whose Side Are You On, Anyway?	46
A Cold Day in Hell	49

Waking Up Dead	52
It Started With the Fishing Boat	56
Sleeping It Off	58
Rescue Me	61
Wait 'Till Your Father Gets Home	65
In a Driverless Car	68
My Family and other Zombies	72
Us Against Them	76
Hair of the Dog	78
The 15th Incarnation	81
Cull	83
Worship	86
Orders	88
The Beginning	91
The Final Party	93
Afterword	96

For Milo

Party Time

Brandon grabbed another beer from the cooler and turned to survey the crowd. He nodded to himself. It was going well. He was happy.

Now, if he could just find a way to get Ashley on her own, he'd be even happier.

He worked his way past the knots of people who had gathered in the kitchen area to talk, and back into the main lounge where the music was playing and some few people were dancing.

Ashley was over by the bedroom door, her glass of wine cupped up by her neck to keep it safely out of the way of gyrating bodies. She was talking with Jess, but that was okay. Jess and Brandon had dated for a while, but it had been years ago: a platonic, early teenage thing that they laughed about now. That she was still his friend gave Brandon confidence that he was an okay kind of boyfriend.

Brandon was halfway across the room, moving around the dancers and swaying to the beat, when Zach blocked his path.

"Josh is here," he shouted, struggling to be heard over the music and chat.

Brandon nodded his understanding. "Cool.

Has he got them?"

Zach nodded, grinning.

"Cool," Brandon repeated. "Now?"

Again the nod.

They parted: Zach moving towards the main door to the apartment where Brandon could see Josh waiting with a large box in his arms; Brandon heading in the other direction, to where his iPod was plugged into the speakers.

"Hey!" he shouted over the groans and protests that greeted the sudden silence. "Hey, everyone! Up to the roof. We've got a surprise!"

He headed back through the crowd which was now grudgingly making its way out and up the stairs. He was able to position himself next to Ashley as he did so, and guided her through the crush with a hand on the small of her back. She gave him a smile and he knew that things were going to be okay.

Up on the roof, Josh was unpacking the box and setting up small devices around the parapet. Central Park was a dark absence in the distance. It would be the perfect backdrop.

"What is it?" Ashley asked Brandon as they found a space to stand in.

Brandon grinned and took a pull on his beer. "Wait and see."

A moment later Josh moved back towards the gathered crowd, unwinding a spool of cable and holding a small box. He looked over at Brandon, who nodded, and then he pressed a button on the box.

The first set of fireworks went off with a whoosh and a second later fire burst in the sky.

There were an assortment of gasps and whoops, and Brandon felt himself tingle as Ashley slipped her arm through his and gazed up at the sky.

Another press of a button and a second set of rockets burst into the sky, lighting up the night.

However, unlike the first set, the light from these fireworks didn't die away. Instead they grew in intensity. The light became almost too bright to look at, and then Brandon realised it wasn't coming from the fireworks but from the sky itself. The dark of the night sky was torn with ribbons of red, like lava running through the atmosphere.

And then fireballs started to fall from the heavens and the assembled enjoyment changed to confusion and panic and, as one, the crowd turned and tried to squeeze through the door.

In the melee, Brandon lost sight of Ashley and then, in a tangle of feet, he fell and lost sight of anything at all.

Stalking

He liked the dark. That was where he lived. Even when he walked in the daylight, talking and joking with friends and colleagues, he existed in a cocoon of darkness.

The night was the time when he could really be himself. No need to hold his desires in check, he could let them spread out far and wide and no-one could see them.

He stood in the shadow of the tree and waited. Sunset came late at this time of day on the Eastern seaboard, but it had finally arrived and he only had the streetlights to contend with.

He watched people walk past on the street and smoked another cigarette. He looked as though he was killing time, but he was waiting for that particular someone.

She came past here every Tuesday at this time, walking back from her Pilates class. He knew where she went and who with.

Always do your homework was his number one rule.

He knew which routes she took and when and why she might change her routine. He knew everything he needed to know.

And he knew that tonight was the night.

Right on schedule she appeared under a distant streetlight. The evening was warm, and she was still in her sweats. He could see the glisten on her skin even from here.

He watched as she approached, counting slowly under his breath, and then as she passed him he stubbed his cigarette on the sole of his shoe and slipped the stub into his pocket with the others. No sense leaving evidence.

From his other pocket he pulled the thin latex gloves on – skin coloured so as not to give anything away – and then he set off after her.

She would turn off the main drag just one block up, and that's where he would take her. There was an alleyway between the school and the track which was always deserted at this time on this day.

He was so intent on following her that he didn't see the sky start to change and ripple. He didn't see the tears which appeared in the firmament.

The first thing he knew was when she glanced to the sky and started to run. He looked up and finally saw what was happening, and just had time to notice the ball of fire which was hurtling towards him.

After that he knew nothing.

Dude

- Wow, look at those stars, dude.
- Don't call me 'dude', Gav; it makes you sound like a dickhead. This is Romford, not fucking Venice Beach.
- Oh, man, chill, 'kay? It's all good. Here, have another toke, dude.
- You are such a spaz.
- Ha. I know. That's why you love me, innit?
- Argh, gettoff. Stop being such a dick.
- Worried someone might see?
- Don't be daft. Who's around, in the middle of nowhere, at this time of the morning?
- Ah, but that's the question.
- What?
- Hmmmm?
- What's the question?
- Sorry?
- I said who was around at this time of the morning, and you said that was the question.
- Well, it is the question, dude.
- What is?
- Is it morning?
- Of course it's fucking morning. It's... well, just after five.

- Ah yes. Five. A lovely number. But is it morning?

- That's why they call it five in the morning, dickhead.

- But we've not been to bed.

- So?

- So, if you've not been to bed, then it's just a late night, innit? I mean, think about it, dude. It's all perception. If you stay up all night, then it just gets later and later until suddenly – bang! – it's morning, and then it's early. But where's the… you know… tipping point thingy.

- Fulcrum.

- Hah, ha, ha. You said cum!

- *Crum*, you dick!

- Oh. Yeah. So, where's that, then? When does late become early. I mean, if I was your mum…

- Leave her out of it.

- Okay, dude. Chill, man. If I was *my* mum, I might go to bed at like, ten thirty, and then if you woke me at midnight, I'd be like – 'who is that at this late hour?' – or whatever. But to you and me, it would be early, cos we'd've, like, only just gone out and that. But if you woke her at four, she'd be all like – 'why did you wake me so early?' – and suddenly we've tipped over. Cos, that might just be late to you and me, cos we'd been up all night. So, is it late or early? That's the question.

- Does it matter? It's five in the morning either way.

- It sure is, dude, and those stars are amazing.

- That, I can agree with.
- Dude?
- What?
- Is it me or is the sky melting?

The Third Time's the Charm

Michael stared at the ceiling, exhausted but still unable to sleep. It was late. Or early. He wasn't sure.

He listened to Debbie's soft breathing and reached down under the covers to stroke his half-erect penis.

It was amazing stuff, this Viagra, he thought. They'd managed twice already and he reckoned he would be good to go again soon.

He remembered nights like this when he was young. In the first flush of a new relationship there would be the getting in to the flat, ripping off the clothes shag. Then there would be the slowly, longer, finally made it to the bed shag. And then, in the middle of the night, there would be the waking together, half-asleep shag. Sometimes there was a morning shag, but other times it would be the recriminating, need to get a bus, 'give me a call sometime, yeah?' goodbye.

Of course, with age and a 'proper' relationship, most of that tended to die away. There was still the occasional impromptu quickie, but mostly it was timetabled: around work, around kids, around TV even. Sex just lost its excitement and became something you did because you'd always done it, like clipping the edges after you mowed the lawn rather than before, or making your toast under the grill rather than in the toaster, because you liked the combination of one side soft, one side crunchy.

And then he'd met Debbie. It had been – oh, three years, really? – and they still had sex like they'd only just met.

That was the beauty of an affair. The adrenaline caused by keeping the secret, and the fact they only got a night together once or twice a year, kept it fresh and exciting. Kept it urgent.

He still loved Marjorie, of course. And from what he could tell, Debbie was still in love with John, but blowing off steam together every now and then allowed them to go home and carry on rather than blowing everything up and trying to start afresh.

That was what Michael told himself, anyway, and at his age starting again was the last thing he wanted to do.

Of course, it wouldn't have worked if Debbie hadn't been married too. He'd thought about an affair on and off over the years, but it had always seemed to be too much trouble. He hadn't wanted to deal with the endless 'when are you going to leave her so we can be together?' conversations that he believed most affairs were plagued by.

Debbie had no more desire to run off with Michael than he with her. It was a mutual arrangement that allowed them both to scratch their itches. And no-one was getting hurt, were they?

His hand, absentmindedly fondling himself as his mind wandered, started to move with a little more urgency as his erection rekindled. He gripped it hard, feeling his pulse moving through it, and then turned in the bed to prod at Debbie's lower back.

She stirred, mumbling something, then her hand came round behind her and took hold of him. She swivelled her body around to face him, her eyes half-lidded and her mouth curled into a smile.

She kissed him gently, and he could taste the staleness of her sleep-mouth, but rather than putting him off, it just made him harder. She stroked him slowly and he moaned into her mouth, then rising up, she pushed him onto his back, straddled him, and sank down in a single movement.

They let out matching groans and started to move together, she lifting and then grinding, he pushing up and pulling down, placing his hands on her hips and guiding her speed.

It was languid and comfortable, but quickly built to a climax. Debbie put her head back and let out a yelp as she shuddered, and that set off Michael's own orgasm. He came hard, and the room seemed to shake around him with a huge roaring and crashing noise.

His erection had dwindled almost immediately and the sleep which had eluded him now threatened to swamp him, but he was aware of Debbie leaping from him and rushing to the window.

"What the fuck was that?" she asked, her voice panicked.

"You mean it wasn't me?"

Uluru

It changes with the light. Never the same. Always something new. A glimpse of the heart, emanating a different beat with every second.

Camira puts down her camera and admires the rock in the afternoon sun as it starts to burn in orange hues. This place is her centre, her core. It is her home and her life, her crib and her grave. It is also her source of income, and for that she says a daily prayer of thanks.

Now is the time, not for film or pixels, but for paint. Her photos of the rock sell around the world to magazines and agencies. She puts in the time and patience to catch as many of the rock's moods as she can, though she knows that she will never catch them all, just as she can never count the stars.

But the paintings are her true love. They sell well, especially to tourists who love the idea of some 'genuine Aboriginal art' ("And she's a woman too!"), but that is a lesser consideration. For her, the times when she channels all that she can see and feel through pigments to canvas, are the times she is truly alive.

She has never gone 'walkabout' or indulged in

'dreamtime' or any of the other clichés that people seem to expect of her. But when she is painting she does sometimes feel as though she is truly communing with her ancestors. She would never tell anybody – she would be too embarrassed, too afraid of fulfilling a stereotype – but sometimes she feels as though she is not the painter at all, but that someone – *someones* – else is doing the work, and she is always as surprised by the finished products as the eager tourists.

It pains her to sell the work, but she needs to live. And her apartment is already too full to think about keeping any more. And yet, at least once a month, she adds a new one to her collection. One more painting which she cannot bring herself to sell. One more painting which is just for her.

She is mixing the orange to the colour of the rock when the sky starts to fall. She looks up at the cataclysm overhead, and around at the fires starting in the brush. Once more she feels the possession of others, a whole family, a whole nation standing alongside her – inside her – guiding her hand. They keep her calm and steady as she adds a little more red to the mix.

Grab the Wheel

It was late when Todd got home from church: nearly eleven. It had been a long evening, but worthwhile and so very fulfilling. It was wonderful to see God's work played out in front of him in such a way. The singing had been uplifting and the healings... oh, yes!

He pulled the Volvo into the drive and climbed out of the car.

It was a quiet evening, and still warm. He stood for a moment and gazed around him, breathing in the faint scent from the sleeping flowers, so much nicer than the exhaust fumes and fast food that he smelt every day in the city. It really was a gift to be allowed to live in such a haven. The other houses on the street were dark, except for Bud Harrigan's opposite. The light burned there at all hours of the night while Bud drank the beer he seemed to have been named for and played his music too loud. Tonight, thankfully, all was quiet, but Todd could see the shape of his neighbour moving through the fully-lit front room.

As though on cue, the thrash of drums and guitars split the night and Todd winced at the raucous sound. And then Bud was at the window, raising a red and white can in salute, and Todd knew that this was a performance for his benefit.

He felt a moment's anger, but then that was replaced by shame. All humans were God's creations – even Bud, he reminded himself – and so worthy of respect. He would simply try to talk to Bud again, to get him to accept God's grace and to reject the devil's music and the accompanying liquor. He would talk to him and try to save him before it was too late.

In the morning, though, he thought. Tonight he would simply use his earplugs as usual and let Bud have his fun.

Todd turned towards his house, but was stopped by a crashing roar as the street was suddenly lit in crimson hues. The sky was shredded with ribbons of red fire and bolts of it started to rain down.

One such bolt, whistling in its passage, raced from behind Todd's house, and he turned to track it as it fell to earth.

An almighty explosion knocked him to the ground.

When he opened his eyes and sat up, shaking the disorientation from his head, he could no longer see Bud's house. It was gone. In its place was a smoking pit lit by the fire within.

Todd struggled to his feet, a beatific smile lifting his features. He stood on one leg and hopped around as he pulled off his left shoe, and then repeated the operation for the right. His socks went next, then his shirt, his trousers and his pants, all in quick succession.

It was happening! It was finally happening!

Todd let out a whoop as he saw the neighbourhood around him burn with righteous fire. The ground started to shake and split around him, but he paid it no heed as he set off, as naked as a newborn, running down the middle of the road.

"I'm here, Lord," he screamed over the cataclysmic noise. "I'm here! Come get me!"

The After Party

Brandon was shaken awake. His bed seemed unusually hard and unyielding, and he was pain from head to foot.

As consciousness reasserted itself, he realised that he wasn't lying in his bed at all, but on some kind of concrete floor. He rolled onto his back, a groan escaping him as his battered body protested the movement, and remembered.

He was still on the roof of his block. The sky above him was a crosshatching of red fire and black smoke. Jets of yellow flame streaked across it as fireballs rained down. And the building itself was the source of the shaking.

Brandon didn't know if it was the impact of the fireballs, or an earthquake, or what, but the surface on which he was lying was shimmying and groaning underneath him.

He had to get down.

He pushed himself to his feet, steadying himself on the doorframe which led back into the building. As he did he remembered tripping as he tried to help Ashley through the crush. He must have been trampled by the others trying to escape. That was why his body felt so bruised.

Ashley!

He looked around him, but there was no sign of her, or of any of the others. They must have escaped. He should find them, find her, and see if they could work out just what the hell was happening.

He lurched through the doorway and was met, almost immediately, by billows of smoke coming up the stairway. Something lower down was on fire. He couldn't go that way.

Instead he made unsteady progress to the edge of the roof and scouted along for the top of the fire escape. The lights had gone out, so he had to search mostly by touch or use the occasional flashes of light from fireballs passing overhead. He glanced up at each one, fearful that it would be heading for him, then continued his search while the light lasted.

Finally his hands closed around the rungs of the ladder and he swung over the side and started to climb down.

Floor after floor, he worked his careful way. The rooms he passed were dark without any signs of life. At the fifth floor, he saw smoke emerging from around the window frame, and as he reached the fourth he could feel the heat of flames.

The third floor was on fire. A fireball had smashed a hole in the wall just six feet to the left of the fire-escape and it had taken a good hold. He turned his face from the flames and hurried down, hoping that his friends, hoping that Ashley, had been able to get past unscathed.

As he descended the final ladder the shaking of the building threatened to throw him from his perch, but he held on with tired and aching hands, and finally felt his feet touch the earth. It was trembling beneath him and, as he took a step forward, a thin crack opened up across the alleyway in front of him.

He stepped over it quickly, before it could widen into something uncrossable, and stumbled out into West 55th Street. He had to find his friends. He had to find Ashley.

Shock and Awe

"Is all in readiness?" squawked General Xorle-Jian-Splein across the bridge to his sub-ordinates.

"Yes, sir," came the unified squeak from the small lizard-like troops who were in charge of the various navigation and weapons systems.

"Good, good," the general rubbed his foreclaws together in a fashion which even he thought looked a little disturbed and over-eager, so he let them drop and then looked around to see if anyone had noticed. They hadn't. All the little newts were paying attention to their screens, as they should. That was good. He wouldn't have to dock any tails. Or heads.

"Are all the weapons armed and targeted?" he asked of one junior officer.

The lizard was too nervous to answer and just shook, nodded, and pointed to its screen.

"Excellent!"

He looked up at the main viewscreen, at the blue green planet nestling in the centre of their crosshairs. He widened his gaze to take in the small winking lights that indicated the rest of the fleet. They were all now in their final positions and waiting for his word to start the attack.

"Those *Earthlings* will never know what hit them," he declared, and then took a deep breath, ready to give the order.

"Erm, sir?" squeaked a tiny newt whose job it was to monitor the planet below for any sign that, despite their numerous countermeasures, the Xulxaxian fleet had been detected.

"What!" Xorle-Jian-Splein roared, annoyed at being interrupted at his big moment.

"S-s-something's happening, s-s-sir." It pointed to the screen.

The general looked up and saw that the view had changed. The blue green sphere, swaddled in ribbons of white cloud, was now a hell-ball of fire, riven with glowing red veins.

"What?" the general gasped, uncomprehending. "What!" He turned on his heel, nearly knocking the tiny newt from its chair with his magnificent tail. He rounded on the weapons officer. "Is that us? Did someone launch prematurely? Come on! Tell me!"

The weapons officer shook its head, trying to read the screen in front of it while bowing its head in obeisance over and over again. "No, sir," it said, "it's just… just… happened."

General Xorle-Jian-Splein was at a loss, not a usual position for him. He entirely failed to behead the weapons office and instead turned back to look at the screen as the planet beneath him burned prematurely. All that destruction and none of it his fault. Oh, he was going to be in trouble for this.

Roadside

The convoy was only two miles outside Sangin when the lead Humvee exploded.

The other three cars all slewed to a halt, blocking the road. No-one shouted 'bomb'. No-one needed to be given instructions. No-one had to think twice about what to do. They had trained for this, over and over, and many of them had been in this situation before.

Corporal Jackson hugged his rifle to his chest and joined the spread of them as they faced outwards from the cars, trying to see any source of attack. A roadside bomb was a great way to start an ambush, but this time there was nothing but the crackling of the burning jeep. Jackson tried not to think about his comrades who had been in the vehicle and kept his sense focussed outwards, waiting for the word that all was safe and they could start to recover the situation.

That was when the second fireball hit, exploding just to the side of the road and throwing dirt up in the air. This was quickly followed by a third. And a fourth. And a fifth.

"Bombardment!" shouted Sergeant Pearce, and Jackson bent, ran towards the relative safety of the vehicle he had to recently left, and dropped down, scanning up and around, trying to find the source of the incoming projectiles.

The sky was crosshatched with black contrails from the incoming fireballs. They were too many to count. Beyond those, the blue of the sky was splitting like the skin of a ripe peach to reveal hell-light from within.

And then the ground underneath them started to quake. Jackson didn't wait for the order. He moved away from the car into the open road. He was just in time, as the road cracked along its length. Jackson leapt out of the way as the crack widened, and then suddenly the convoy, and most of his fellows soldiers were gone, disappearing down into the growing gorge. Despite the danger, the fire from the skies, the shaking of the earth beneath his boots, he moved to the edge to look down. He could see nothing. The day had lost its brightness, but that was not the problem. The crack was wide and deep and seemed to extend down to the centre of the earth, like a fracture in the very mantle.

And then, very faintly, Jackson saw the light of an explosion and, in silhouette, the shape of one of the jeeps. It looked like a toy.

He moved back from the edge and looked around. The convoy was gone. His squad was gone. Most of the road was gone too. He watched, heedless of the danger, as the sky grew still darker and the flames bloomed in a desert increasingly split by new ravines. He had no way to know if this was happening just here or everywhere, but he could feel that this was it. Finally. After this, everything would be gone.

He cradled his rifle and started to jog back towards the town. He kept one eye on the sky and one eye on the ground, watching for hazards. He would find what shelter he could. When this ended, if it ended, people might need someone with his skills.

And, if it didn't end. Well, it didn't matter then, did it?

They Rise

Pont d'Iéna shook under Jean-Patrique's feet as he crossed it, dodging the few fireballs which were still falling. In front of him, a tangle of metal marked where the Eiffel Tower had been standing the last time he'd been here. But he didn't care about any of those things. He couldn't afford to. Finding somewhere safe, somewhere with a lockable door, was all that mattered.

The Trocadero station had provided perfect shelter from what had been rumoured to be happening on the surface. But when the shaking of the earth had threatened to bury them all, Jean-Patrique had been swept up with the other early morning/late night passengers, and carried to the surface; out into a city he barely recognised.

He had raced, along with many of his fellow travellers, into the park, towards the river and away from the burning, toppling buildings.

That was when the earth started to split and trees started to crash around them. One or two of the others were crushed, but Jean-Patrique swerved and dodged and headed for the river. At least there, there would be nothing to fall on him.

The crash of the toppling Tower was almost

lost in the roar from the earth, but there was no mistaking the shock wave which rippled through the ground and knocked Jean-Patrique on his back.

He struggled to his feet and stumbled to the Avenue which ran alongside the Seine. He ran to the wall, out from under the threat of collapsing trees, and there he paused to look around. He could see fires and wreckage everywhere. The only intact structure in sight was the bridge which had somehow survived.

He had no desire to cross, however. It looked like a bad idea. But then he heard a new noise behind him.

It was surprising he heard it over the noise of the city collapsing, but the low groan cut through the cloud of sound, ran straight down and his spine and sent his legs running along and over the bridge. He didn't even look back to see what it was that he had heard. He didn't want to know. He just wanted to find shelter before they caught him. Before they caught him and…

He ran and he didn't look back.

Eternal Love

Margaret adjusted the plastic tube from the nebulizer so it fit more comfortably under her nose, then dropped her hands back down to the bed. She wrapped them around one of Bob's and gave a gentle squeeze.

She had no way to know if he was aware of her. He hadn't opened his eyes or said anything all night, but she believed he could feel her and take comfort from her presence. She had spent over sixty years at his side, and she wanted him to know she wasn't going to leave now, no matter what happened.

From the sounds she could hear, the world outside the hospital was coming to a violent end. There had been explosions and screams, and now the building itself was shaking itself apart. But here, in this room, her world had already been ending and she didn't have time for anything else.

She'd made him promise that she could leave first; that he wouldn't leave her alone; but it seemed this was one promise he wasn't going to be able to keep.

His breath was hitching hard, despite the hissing mask over his face, and with each pause she wondered if it would be his last.

"It's okay, love," she said to him, just loud enough to be heard over the noise of the world ending. "It's okay. I'm here. And I don't mind. You can go. I won't be far behind you."

She had been saying this to him all day. It had nothing to do with the cataclysm that seemed to be tearing through the outside world. It was more to do with her high blood pressure, the extra oxygen she needed, and the cancer which was eating its way out of her lungs and into the rest of her body.

She listened to his harsh breathing as it grew still more ragged and the pauses between grew longer, and she waited.

Finally, the shaking and the noises outside seemed to fade away, and with it so did Bob's stentorious respiration. It slowly wound down to silence, and then, without fanfare, it stopped.

Margaret let out a sigh, then drew in a ragged breath of her own. Tears didn't come. She had already grieved for this moment. All that was left was relief.

She struggled to her feet and took the single step which brought her to the edge of his bed, her oxygen tank rolling at her heel. She braced her hands on either side of her beloved, and then bent to kiss his forehead.

She straightened and gazed at his face. "Goodnight, my love. See you soon."

Bob opened his eyes.

Margaret reeled backwards with a gasp and collapsed into her chair.

He removed his mask and sat up.

"Mags?" he said.

She simply stared at him in disbelief.

"What happened, Mags?" He turned his hands in front of his face, examining them. "What happened? I feel amazing!"

Margaret's mouth goldfished for a moment before she found her voice. "You died," she told him.

He stared at her for a moment, then nodded. "Yes. I guess I did. That would explain a lot. And the hunger."

"Hungry, love?" she asked, still finding it hard to believe she was having this conversation.

"Oh yes. So very, very hungry."

"What do you want?"

He stared at her, licking his lips, and finally she held out her hand to him. "Will it hurt?" she asked.

He nodded. "But not for long. And then… it's fantastic."

She rose once more from her chair, and took the step back to the bed. There, she leant forward until she could collapse against him. She hugged him tight and only screamed a little. Then, after a moment's darkness, it was all so much better.

P. O. V.

dark very dark black in fact completely black nothing to see nothing to hear dead completely dead completely black and completely dead and soft soft material all around soft material and hard hard black dark black completely dead black hard under soft under dark under ground kick the dark kick the black kick the hard harder harder harder hardest black dark moving black shredding soft breaking hard digging side digging out side soil and black and dark and out in earth in soil in ground and out and out and up and up and up and up and out and air to breath or not to breathe but dark and air and night and out and hunger and shaking and fire and dark and night and people and hunger and dark and dark and hunger and running and hunger and out and hunger and people and running and black and him yes him oh him smell him taste him eat him and dark so very dark

The Hangover

Broadway was deserted. The boards in Times Square were blank. The fireballs had stopped, and the quakes had calmed down to an occasional aftershock. But with the city crumbling around him, New York was still a dangerous place to be, but Brandon couldn't leave. Not yet. Not without Ashley.

Buildings had been fracturing and tumbling behind him as he ran. Cracks had opened in the sidewalk, in the blacktop, but he had leapt over them and kept on running. He wasn't sure where he was going, at first, but then he decided that Ashley's apartment would be the place to start. He hadn't planned to take in the sights, but it was the quickest way to her place off 5th Avenue.

He had headed straight to the park, to get out from under the threat of falling masonry, and then cut across. Okay, yes, he could have stayed in the park all the way up to 5th, but by heading down 7th he'd been able to try and answer a question which had started to niggle him.

Where was everyone?

He didn't think he had been out on the roof for that long, and a lot of people must have been hurt by the bombardment and the quakes. It had been about midnight when they went to light the fireworks, so many people would have been inside, in bed. But this was New York. Never sleeping was more or less the city's reason for being. So, where was everyone? Had they really had a chance to flee? Or had they been swallowed by the earth?

It wasn't quite the quickest route. But he felt he needed to look at the heart of the city. He needed to see the sights and find anyone else he could.

The area was deserted, however, and he couldn't see why. There were a few body parts – he tried not to look too closely at them – but nothing like the carnage he would have expected.

He stood in the middle of the most famous square in the world and, for a moment, Ashley was no longer in his mind. Instead it was filled with the utter stillness of the ever-beating heart of this insomniac city.

And then a low moan echoed across the empty square. It raised the hairs on the back of Brandon's neck. He'd always thought that was a cliché, but it turned out that there was truth in the myth.

He turned slowly, and finally he saw someone. Many someones, actually. A whole avenue full of someones.

Some were burned, some had been crushed, others bore bite marks on necks and faces, still others had different wounds, or no wounds at all. These last were almost uniformly dressed in soil-stained suits and dresses and looked even more dead than those who had been freshly injured.

Brandon was young and had seen all the right TV and films. He didn't need to wait to be told that this was a zombie horde he was facing. He simply turned and ran.

Writing The End

Early morning walks had always been part of the routine, but this had been anything but a routine morning.

Owen was always up and out by 4.30am. He walked through Rusholme and did a couple of laps of Platt Fields before heading back and reaching his desk at 6.00. He would write for two hours, then shower, then go to work. Home again at 6.30 he would eat his tea, drink a couple of swift double vodkas, and hit the sack by 9.00. The next morning it would start all over again.

Whenever he would finish a novel, he would take a week off and allow himself a few late nights with friends and a trip to the cinema, and then he would take an early night, set the alarm, and start all over again.

In just over two years, he had managed to complete fourteen novels. None of them had been published, but then none of them had ever been sent out. He printed each manuscript, allowed himself to look at it, then he would slip it into a fresh box file and put it on the shelf with the others.

One day, he told himself. One day he would

have the guts to send one to an agent or a publisher. But for now there was no need. If no-one else saw them, they would remain perfect for ever. If they were never rejected, then he could never be a failure. If he didn't send them out, he could be a writer for ever.

This morning, of course, had been different. He had been in the middle of the park when the fireballs started raining down. Somehow, he had remained unscathed, simply watching as the world around him burst into flames.

When the ground had started to shake he had done nothing more brave than to curl into a ball in the middle of the path to wait it out.

As it calmed, he climbed back to his feet and started to walk unsteadily from the park. Maybe he could get home. Maybe it would be as undamaged as he was. Maybe he could still do his writing. He didn't know about going into work, but maybe that part of his day could still be rescued.

He saw the first zombie before he was even halfway back across the park. Its signature lurch was obvious and easily identified.

This time he had a more active reaction. He ran for the shelter and hid.

He cowered there as the undead appeared and disappeared in front of him, and he realised that there would be no writing today and certainly no work. You don't go into work when the world is coming to an end.

And then, as the sun rose, and he could make out the blasted shape of the world, he realised something. Not everything had to come to an end.

He dipped into his pocket and pulled out the notebook he always carried with him on his walks. He grabbed his pen from his inside pocket and started to write. It wasn't the fiction he normally worked on, but a factual account of the world as it now was. Finally, he could write, and there would no longer be any pressure to publish, as there were probably no longer any publishers.

He didn't know if there would be anyone else writing about this, but he didn't care. With no publishers, no distributors, no bookshops, no books and no readers, what he wrote could remain perfect forever.

Owen grinned to himself, then bent his head over his notebook and set about writing the end of the world.

Whose Side Are You On, Anyway?

The quakes had settled back to a vague trembling before Jackson regained the town. The heat of the day and his steady jog had caused sweat to coat his body, but he didn't slow. He had to regain the base, discover what was happening, and see what orders might be waiting for him.

As he ran between the first buildings, he raised his arm to wipe the sweat from his eyes with his sleeve, and as a result he nearly missed the man running towards him.

Just in time, he saw him – the first other human he had seen since the bombardment began – and as his brain registered the vest, his legs were already propelling him into a dive.

With a scream and a shout of, "Allahu Akbar," the man raised his arms and detonated the explosives he was wearing.

The blast wave caught Jackson while he was still in mid-air, and he was blown against the side of a building. He cracked his head and for a moment the world spun around him.

He rolled onto his front and pushed himself

up onto his knees, then took a moment to check himself over and wipe his face with both hands. He seemed to be uninjured, so he slowly regained his feet.

The road was a mess. Those parts of the bomber which hadn't been vaporised, were scattered to the margins. The head, still intact, was lying up against the wall of the building opposite.

Jackson waited, but no-one came to investigate the noise. As he looked around he realised the town had suffered badly under the rain of fireballs, and the quakes had done a good job of finishing the job. He still couldn't understand where the rest of the people could have gone. There couldn't have been just him and the one lone bomber left.

And then a hand grabbed his right ankle.

Jackson jerked back and looked down. He hadn't noticed anyone creeping up, and now he realised why. It was the hand of the bomber. It was no longer attached to anything, but it had animated and grasped at him, perhaps attempting to finish the job the rest of him had started.

With a grunt of disgust, Jackson used his left foot to scrape it off him. And then he stamped on it and ground it into the dirt as the fingers tried to grab and grasp.

Finally, it stopped moving. When Jackson looked up again, he was faced by the missing members of the town. They were clearly dead, but they were still walking towards him, emerging slowly from between the buildings as though the explosion had served as a *muezzin*.

Jackson gaped. The rifle strapped across his chest was forgotten. He simply watched as the crowd advance on him.

The sharp rattle of rifle fire made him jump. His action was matched by the leading figures of the crowd as they jumped and jerked in response to bullet impacts.

A hand grabbed his elbow and Jackson turned, finally remembering to raise his own rifle, but he stopped when he saw it was Sergeant Pearce.

"Come on, lad. Staying here's not going to be good for your health."

Jackson stared at his commanding officer: at the scorched, suppurating burn where the man's hair used to be; at the blackened hole where his right eye used to be; at the bloody mess that used to be the man's left arm.

"Sarge?" he managed to say. "You were hit by a fireball. I thought you were dead."

The sergeant gave a short laugh like a bark. "I am, lad. You didn't think that would stop me, did you? Now come on, the others are waiting."

A Cold Day in Hell

The ice was burning.

McMurdo Station had been struck in several places, and snow was swirling in through the gaps in the roofs. Other fireballs had stuck into the ice and continued to burn, the pools of melting snow failing to extinguish them.

The shaking had fractured the rocks and one or two of the buildings had fallen into the resulting canyons.

Andersen and Heaton held on tight, keeping their position on the slope next to their equipment. They watched the destruction of the base on the plateau beneath them with their fingers locked into cracks in the rocks, and muttered prayers under their breath that they wouldn't be hit or dislodged.

As the quakes calmed, and the immediate peril abated, Heaton glanced across at his Danish research partner. "What the fuck was that?"

"You think I should know? What do you think it was?"

"Fucked if I know. No volcanos in Utah."

Andersen's brow wrinkled. "Yes there are. I believe there are five distinct fields."

"Big enough to do that?"

"No, b-"

"Then shut the fuck up."

"You swear too much."

"Too fucking right, buddy."

"Are you sure it was a volcano?"

"Fireballs raining down? An earthquake big enough to swallow whole buildings? What else could it have been? And, anyway, who's the seismologist here?"

"As far as I know, neither of us is. Though, if I am correct, you have had some small experience in the subject, Although, seemingly, it was insufficient for you to be able to remember that there are five fields in your own home state."

"I swear too much? You talk too fucking much. If you're so clever, which volcano do you think it was? Something close?"

Andersen looked around at the fires dotting the ice, and the dark, steaming ravines in the rock. "Something of this size? I doubt Erebus could have done it."

"You know what I think? You know which volcano I think it was?"

"No, my friend, I do not."

Heaton pulled one hand free from the rocks and pointed a well-gloved finger to the sky which was filling with soot and streamers of burning ash. "All of them," he said.

He drew breath, preparing to say something else, but then stopped when a fresh quake struck.

He plunged his hand back into the crack, holding on tight as the mountain tried to shake them from its back.

The ground below the base gave an ear-rending crack, and split even wider. Andersen and Heaton gaped as rock and ice flew into the air in a cloud.

And then, as they watched, a shape started to appear from within the cloud.

"Holy fucking Jesus," said Heaton. "What the fuck is that?"

Waking Up Dead

When Darren woke, he presumed he was dead.

It was the second time he'd emerged from sleep — or at least unconsciousness — the first being by what he had at first thought were fireworks. He had stumbled to the window, grumbling. Who the hell was setting off fireworks at — he had glanced at the red glow of his bedside clock — five o'clock in the bloody morning?

"What is it, babes?" Shelly had murmured from under the duvet.

"Not sure. Damn kids or something."

He had pulled back the curtains in time to see a fireball hit and destroy Malky's house.

"What the —" was all he had managed to say before the floor disappeared beneath him and all went black.

When he woke for a second time, it was to wracking pain, utter darkness and a burning heat. He had to be dead and this had to be hell.

"Daz?" Shelly asked, and then her voice was swamped by coughing.

Darren lifted his head and looked for her.

"Shell?" he asked, and then started coughing himself as smoke filled his lungs.

Looking across the room he realised he could see. A small amount of light was coming from a line of flame which was lapping at the bottom of his bedroom door. He was still in his house, and it was on fire.

He sat up, his body protesting through the bruises, and pulled off the t-shirt he wore as a pyjama top. He put it over his mouth, and struggled to his feet. He made his way to the bed and felt around for Shelly.

He let out a small yelp as her hand closed over his, then pulled the shirt away from his mouth long enough to speak. "We have to get out. Fire. Come on."

He pulled her from the bed and they stumbled towards the door.

They hadn't even reached it when he stopped. He could feel the heat baking from the door and the flames were licking higher.

The smoke was getting through the t-shirt, and Shelly was almost bent double, hacking it up from her lungs. Darren didn't say anything, but simply turned and started pulling her towards the window. He hoped to God the herbaceous border had grown thick enough to break their fall.

He pulled back the curtains and lifted the window, and stopped. Where there should have been a street, there was a blank rock face.

"What the hell?" he mumbled through the t-shirt.

He stuck his head out into the small gap

between window and rock and looked down and up. The air was clearer, but the view was gloomy and hard to distinguish. The base of his house disappeared down into darkness, as did either side.

Looking up, he could see a crack of dawn-lit sky.

He took a deep breath and pulled his head back inside. "Up," he said to Shelly, pointing to make her understand. "We have to climb."

He had only managed to get his foot onto the windowsill, when the house rocked and shifted under him, knocking him and Shelly from their feet.

As he lay on his back, he could see the rock face passing in front of the window as the floor rocked underneath him.

Then the room was flooded with early morning sunlight as they emerged from the ground and climbed up into the air.

Darren crawled back to the window and looked out. His neighbourhood was blasted and ruined and disappearing down into the distance as the house rose up and up. He gripped the sill and peered out. Looking down he could see a dark shape upon which the house seemed to be balanced. It was growing out of the crack in the ground, and for a moment Darren had thoughts of beanstalks and giants.

But then the view tilted and Darren was looking straight down.

He flew backwards from the window as the

house plummeted towards the ground. He reached out for Shelly's hand and closed his eyes. This time, he knew, he wouldn't be waking up at all.

It Started With the Fishing Boat

The fireballs hit the water with a hiss and a geyser of steam, but the ocean absorbed the swells from their impact. When the quakes hit, no-one on the boat knew, the ocean swallowed those as well.

The living dead might learn to swim given time, but there was not going to be enough of it for them to bother the boat.

So, all in all, the advent of the apocalypse passed the fishermen almost completely by.

But when the head of the beast crested, and the maw opened, they finally saw that the end was upon them. It was their last sight.

Matsuto was lost in his *Ultraman* manga. As the train sped through the Japanese countryside his fellow passengers stirred in consternation, he turned the page and continued to read. When the train rocked and rolled on bucking tracks, he rode the waves and continued to read. Somehow the train managed to coast its way into the centre of Tokyo, but it stopped a mile short of the station as buildings crashed and burned around it. The other travellers crowded against the windows, or pushed towards the doors, unsure if leaving the train was the safer option or maybe suicide. Matsuto ignored the commotion and continued to read.

It was only when a shadow fell over the train that Matsuto realised that the lights inside had gone out. He looked up in annoyance and finally noticed that the people who had been sat around him had vanished.

He twisted in his seat and surveyed the carriage. It was empty.

His brow furrowed in confusion and he glanced back down at his manga. No, it was definitely too dark to continue reading. Something was blocking the light. He leant over to look out of the window. He looked out and up. And up. And up. And up. And a small whimper leaked from his mouth. His manga fell to the floor, unheeded, and he started to scrabble from his chair.

He just had time to utter the word, "Gojira," before the foot of a gigantic lizard descended onto the carriage roof, squashing it and everything in it completely flat.

The gargantuan monster didn't even notice that it had stood on something, but simply considered its march across the city.

Sleeping It Off

Brandon was cold and tired. The floor of the video shop was probably not the most comfortable place to sleep in Montclair, but it was one of the few completely intact buildings he'd found already abandoned and empty. He was unlikely to be disturbed here, either by the curious living or the resident dead.

He hadn't been able to detour via Ashley's apartment. He had had no choice but to run down any street or alleyway that was not packed with the crawling, shambling, lurching corpses that were crowding Lower Manhattan.

He had still tried to wend his way back towards her place, even as the day wound on into night, but had little luck. And then he turned a corner and was faced with a giant lizard's foot, thirty feet wide, plunging towards him. He dived out of the way, and it smashed into the roadway where he'd been, then it carried on past him, kicking the frontages out of a row of coffee shops and restaurants.

The zombies had freaked him out, but this terrified him. He ran, blindly, relying solely on his feet and the concept of 'away'. Ashley had faded from his mind, and he just wanted to find somewhere safe, if such a place still existed.

He was grateful the lights were still on in the Lincoln Tunnel. He'd read *The Stand* and had no desire to go through that experience.

New Jersey was not the haven he had hoped. The apocalypse wasn't, it turned out, just a New York problem – which he was slightly ashamed to admit to himself was a thought that had passed through his mind. He knew it was typical New York hubris, but it still didn't make it any better. And it didn't make the rest of the world any safer.

The zombies were fewer here, and from time to time he thought he saw faces behind the curtains in the windows of the damaged houses he passed.

He raided supermarkets when he was hungry, but so often found the corpses stirring around him as he loaded bags with food and water, that he had taken to selecting smaller shops, and he searched them first.

In contradiction of his expectations, most of the zombies didn't seem that violent. It seemed to depend how long dead they were, and how much brain remained. And he guessed it was also conditional on how violent they had been in life.

The, well, he could only think of them as 'Godzillas' were a different matter. But while he had seen half a dozen parading through New York, towering over the skyline, he had yet to see any on this side of the river.

Finally, he had found a well-stocked, empty, and un-ransacked shop here in Montclair. The empty video shop had provided a secure bolthole and one which other survivors wouldn't think to visit. It was secure, but the small windows and thick walls meant that it was cold. The concrete floor only exacerbated that and proved to be a very hard mattress. He had padded it with coats and sweaters he had found in a nearby shop, but they really didn't do much.

He had spent quite a lot of time cursing his high-school education. Heroes of the Civil War and trigonometry were all very well, but they didn't help you survive the end of the world.

And now, over a week after the first fireball hit, he was huddled in the corner as dawn arrived. He was shivering, yawning, and facing another breakfast of cold, canned food.

He was reaching for the can opener when there was a knocking from the front of the shop. He jumped and dropped the utensil and stared at the blank boards of the door, waiting for whoever it was to go away.

"Brandon?" said a voice. "Hey, buddy? Brandon? Hey, you in there?"

Rescue Me

Six shots and the gun was silenced as the hammer fell on an empty cylinder. Nathan flipped it open and dumped the shells as he dipped his hand into the pouch hanging from his belt for more bullets.

It was empty.

"Shit," he said, and slid his gun back into his holster.

It was funny, he'd always thought that it would be zombies that finally got him. They'd grab him and bite him and chew him and the next thing he knew, he'd be one of them. He'd wondered which kind he'd be: the brainless, drooling, starving kind, or the type which seemed little different to the living, except for their lack of pulse and a slightly more extensive hunger.

He had never thought that it would be other survivors that would bring him down, but that seemed to be the case.

He should have known. Texas was always a land of independence, and that often meant getting together with your friends to keep out the strangers, the different, the others. It had suited him fine in the old world, but in this one he just hadn't been able to form a big enough group – or any group at all – and a lone man was never going to last long.

The leader of the gang facing him straightened up from the half-crouch he had adopted when Nathan started shooting. He looked around him, to see who of his friends was still standing, and nodded.

He pointed to the two bodies on the floor. "Cut their heads off," he said, absently.

It was the only way to stop them coming back. Nathan knew at least that much.

Then the guy looked at Nathan. "They were good men," he said, pointing to the bodies which were currently undergoing a finally fatal mutilation at the hands of their former friends. "You're going to pay for that."

They had been waiting outside the store when Nathan came out. He knew the dynamic before a word was said. It was the same as it had been in the playground when he was in the first grade. The bigger kids would always find a way to take what they wanted from anyone they considered vulnerable.

"I think you'll find that's our food you're stealing," the lead guy had said, and Nathan hadn't waited, but just opened fire.

What he hadn't realised was that the rest of his ammunition was still in his pack, upstairs in the barn he had adopted as a base. Six had been enough to drop two of them, but there were at least another twenty, and now that his gun was plainly empty, there was no way he was going to be able to scare them off.

All he could do was try and find a way to get past them, and run.

He scanned for an escape route, but before he could do anything, a thin blonde woman slipped her way through the crowd and placed her hand on the leader's shoulder.

The man's eyebrows went up in surprise. "Who?" was all he managed to say before the woman slipped a long knife into his belly, twisted, and left him dying in the road.

Two of the others went for her, but she span on her foot and kicked both of them in the head, one after the other, hard enough to knock them from their feet and to take a couple of the others down with them.

She didn't pause, but leapt forward and grabbed Nathan's hand. She pulled him through the suddenly reticent crowd, holding the few braver souls back with her knife.

The reached open space and she said just one word, "Run," and then, still holding his hand, she emulated the word and they headed out of town.

There was a sound of pursuit, but it quickly died away. Nathan presumed none of them was really that keen to catch up with someone who could dispatch their leader so easily.

Eventually, she allowed them to slow their pace. "I hope you got some food in that place, otherwise this was a waste of time."

Nathan nodded and hefted his bag.

"Good. So where are we going?"

He pointed in the direction of his barn, but then stopped.

"Just hang on one minute. Who the hell are you?" he asked.

She stuck out her hand and he couldn't help but notice the blood slicked across it. "Candy. You?"

"Nathan."

"Cool. Shall we go?"

"Hold on. I need to ask. What were you back in the world, some kind of special ops agent? An assassin?"

Candy gave a crooked smile. "Course not. I was a hooker. But you have to be able to look after yourself. And that guy who was about to kill you? He was always a shit, but in this world I could finally do something about it."

She pointed down the road in the direction Nathan had indicated. "Now, come on," she said, "and don't get any ideas or you'll be joining him." She set off walking.

Nathan followed.

Wait 'Till Your Father Gets Home

"Hurry up and finish your breakfast, then its school time."

"Aw, Mum! Do we have to?" said Harry.

"Yes, you do. It's Monday, after all, and it's not a holiday."

"But, Mum! There aren't any schools any more. That's what you said," said Chloe.

"There might not be, but that shouldn't stop us. You still need to learn and your father and I are perfectly capable of teaching you."

"But, Mum!" the children chorused.

"Shush, now and finish your cereal. If you argue any more, I'll tell your father when he gets home and you'll have to answer to him."

That silenced both children. They didn't want to upset Dad. Not any more.

They ate their cereal without saying another word. They didn't even complain about eating it with UHT milk, for once, which was a relief to Sandra.

Eventually, as he scraped up the last of his coco puffs, Harry spoke again, but this time in a normal voice without his earlier whine. "Where's Dad been, Mum? Has he been out all night again?"

Sandra stopped wiping the kitchen side and turned to answer the question. She felt it was important to answer all questions about Brian as fully and truthfully as possible. It was the only way they were going to get through this.

"Yes, you know he goes out at night. He goes to try and find food for us – the food that you eat. He's keeping us alive in the midst of all this… turmoil, and you should be very grateful."

"Why does he only go out at night, Mum?"

"He does it so he can spend all day with you. Because he loves you," Sandra told them. It was an answer, and it was true, but in this case, she felt it was okay to keep the completely full and true answer from her children.

The full and true answer would have been that it was safer for Brian to go out at night. At night he was less conspicuous and so had a better chance of making it back home alive.

"When does he sleep?" Harry asked.

"Whenever he needs to," replied Sandra in the tone of voice which said that she was not open to answering further questions.

She was rescued from further quizzing by the sound of the front door opening.

"Hi, honey, I'm home!" Brian shouted. It was an old joke between them that had turned into a routine.

He walked into the kitchen and was carrying three carrier bags full of assorted tinned and packaged food.

"All okay?" Sandra asked.

Brian nodded. "Of course it was!" he said in a hearty voice. Then he half-turned away from the children and showed her his left hand. The middle finger was hanging strangely: obviously broken.

"Oh no," she said in a low voice. "Not again."

Brian shrugged and nodded. "Yeah, sorry. It was carrying the bags. I caught it and – boom – it just went."

Sandra sighed and opened the kitchen drawer, taking out a pair of gardening secateurs. She took hold of his cold hand, and with only a slight grimace, snipped off the offending digit, leaving just two and the thumb.

"Okay?" she asked him.

He held the hand up in front of his face and flexed it, examining for a moment the dried stumps. "Yep. Fine. Thank you." He leant forward to kiss her cheek and she let him.

"You'll have to be more careful, you know."

"Yes, dear," he said; another old joke. Then he turned to the children. "Right, Maths this morning, I think," he said in an enthusiastic voice, and both children groaned.

In a Driverless Car

Todd had managed to find some clothes, though it had taken him a couple of days. Although it was warm in Wichita this time of year, he'd still managed to get a cold from sleeping rough for two nights. Now, weeks later, he'd still not managed to shake it off.

He'd set up home in Walmart's camping department. It had everything he needed, and there were lots of places to hide when scavengers passed through. Sometimes they were human, sometimes they were zombie. To Todd they were just interruptions to his despair.

When the fireballs stopped falling, and the earth stood still, and the monsters started striding across the earth, Todd waited and waited and waited. And God never came.

After he'd found the Walmart, and some clothes, he'd hidden away and tried to understand. His illness had left him debilitated, but he suspected it was more a malaise of the spirit than the flesh.

He had seen the world come to an end. Whole swathes of people seemed to have disappeared – far more than the natural and unnatural disasters could account for – but he had been left behind.

How had God allowed that to happen?

He had spent hours inside his tent, wrapped in blankets and comforters from the bedding department, and tried to understand.

In the end he had come down to two possible options.

In the first, it had indeed been the rapture. The faithful had been snatched up even as the fire rained down. But Todd had obviously not had enough faith, not enough belief, or had done something to anger God sufficiently to leave him behind. Had he been too proud, of his house, his family, his faith? Had his anger at Bud and his loud music been so great it had excluded him from paradise? Had he felt lust, or gluttony, or any of the other sins?

With an honesty engendered by the end of the world, Todd could only answer 'yes' to all of the questions he posed. He had been a sinner, he realised, far worse than the ones he castigated or picketed against. He deserved to be shunned.

But another thought intruded in amongst the shivering and the self-recrimination. At first it was nothing more than a notion, but it took hold and, like the virus that was causing his temperature and his cough, it blossomed.

What if – it still made him pause whenever the thought percolated through his mind – what if there was actually no God? What if there was no God, no heaven, no rapture? What if there was nothing more than a ball of rock, floating through space, carrying an infestation called mankind; an infestation that had brought about its own destruction? What if everything he had believed had been wrong?

It was this thought, Todd suspected, that was prolonging his cold and making it worse. How could he recover from anything when that thought was festering in his mind?

He was once more locked in this cycle of thinking when he heard the noises. He realised that he had been hearing them for some time, but had only just become aware of them. There were people in the store, people in the camping department, and his small electric light was shining like a beacon to bring them – whether human or zombie – closer.

He quailed for a moment, and then something like resolve gripped him.

He didn't know which of his options was correct. Either there was a God, and Todd had been shut out of his mercy; or there was no God at all and nothing mattered. Either way, it seemed he was on his own. And whoever it was out there was going to find him this time. That much was a fact. He could sit in his tent and wait for them to come and find him, or he could do something about it.

He gritted his teeth and let the blankets fall away from his shoulders. He reached down and gripped the handle of the hunting knife he had secured for himself. Then with the closest thing to a battle cry that he could muster, he launched himself from the tent, finally master of his own fate.

My Family and other Zombies

Margaret was thoroughly enjoying her afterlife. It wasn't, of course, quite what she had expected, but to some extent it was better.

She and Bob had always been vaguely religious. They liked carols, that was true, and most of the ordinary hymns. Christmas and Easter were obligatory church days, and sometimes she would decide that they should go along on this Sunday or that. It was how she'd been brought up. How they'd both been brought up. But she'd never actually given it much thought.

She knew from the news that people got into an awful pother about religion, but she'd never understood that. She figured there was probably something out there, something that liked people to get together and sing to it slowly and loudly. It liked you to be nice to people – something Margaret had always been inclined to do anyway – and it preferred it if you weren't nasty or dirty.

That all sounded fine to Margaret and she didn't see what all the fuss could be about.

In all that, she'd never really given much

thought to what happened after you died. She remembered Sunday school lessons where she learned about eternal paradise and St Peter and pearly gates, but she'd always rather suspected that that was nothing more than optimistic bunkum. Rather, she thought, it was more likely that when you died you just, well, stopped. That had never worried or scared her. Especially in the last few years it had seemed like a nice notion. There had been days when she would have been quite happy to just, well, stop.

After all, eternity sounded like an awfully long time.

But this, well, she knew she wasn't really alive, but in many ways it was better. All her aches and pains had gone — even her dicky hip felt better — and she had more energy than she could remember having since she was very little. Admittedly the world had gone to hell, but then Bob had been predicting that for years. Oh, and alive people seemed to run away from them when they saw them. But every silver lining had its cloud, as her mother had said.

They had left the hospital as soon as it stopped shaking and had headed home. Their house had been flattened, but Margaret was surprised to find that she wasn't that upset. It was just a place, just one of many they had lived in. What did it matter as long as they had their health, she joked to Bob, who laughed longer than it was worth.

They rescued some clothes and a couple of mementoes from the rubble, and then they decided to just wander wherever the notion took them. When they had both been young enough to really enjoy their lives, they had both been too busy with work and children to actually do so. Now, there was no pressure, no rules, few other people, and – it seemed – all the time in the world.

Bob had decided they should go and visit their daughter, and Margaret hadn't had a decent reason to refuse. Many roads were impassable to cars, but that didn't bother them. They could walk, now, and they felt like walking too. And what did it matter how long it took them to get from Southampton to Leeds? It wasn't like they had an appointment.

Old habits had died hard, and they had started off walking up the motorway. But after a while they realised that it wasn't the quickest way if you were on foot, and anyway it was just plain dull.

So instead they had started to cut across country, wandering through farmland, woods, small villages and larger towns.

It was like a road trip only without roads, Bob had joked, and Margaret had laughed until she would have cried, if she could anymore.

They went largely unmolested by others. The whole country seemed deserted. But they were crossing a major road not far from Oxford when they heard the voice.

"You there! You! You dirty fucking zombies!

Stop where you are! Come any closer and we'll chop you into small pieces and burn you up!"

Bob and Margaret both stopped in the middle of the A34 and looked around. The voice had come from the trees and, sure enough, a figure emerged. It was hard to make him out in the early morning mists, but Margaret had a strange moment of recognition which grew stronger as the figure approached.

Finally he was close enough to see properly and Bob burst out laughing. "Jim, you old bastard, what are you doing here?"

Jim smiled and the two men shook hands and clapped shoulders. "Same as you, I reckon. Heading north on a family hunt."

Bob and Margaret both nodded.

"Is the wife with you?" Bob asked, and Jim nodded, waving a hand towards the trees where a woman had appeared. She hurried down to join the crowd amid hugs and cheek-kisses.

"All zombied up, I see," Bob commented as they set off walking again.

"Of course. It's the only way to be."

"It surely is."

They walked in silence for a moment and then Margaret pointed to the road sign pointing into Oxford. "Well, this deserves a celebration. Shall we pop into the city and find someone to eat?"

Us Against Them

"Where the fuck did you get all this from?" Jackson asked, as the zombie formerly-known-as Sergeant Pearce climbed down from the cab.

The truck he had arrived in was the lead vehicle in a convoy of twelve open-backed lorries. Each one was stacked high with weaponry – rifles and pistols and machine guns, as you might expect, but also shoulder-mounted SAMs, RPGs, flamethrowers and other things Jackson couldn't identify.

The pale form of his commanding officer grinned and Jackson fought the chill that ran down his spine despite the heat of the day.

"Some from stockpiles. Some from bases. And quite a lot from them." He pointed to the drivers of the other trucks. They were all also zombies. And they were all former-Taliban. It had turned out that death really was the great leveller. Finding themselves dead but still moving, and with bodies which wouldn't heal if they were damaged, the radicalism had faded very quickly.

"Insurgent weaponry?" Jackson asked.

Pearce shook his head and placed a cold hand on Jackson's shoulder. "No, son. Just weaponry."

"Okay. So what's it all for?"

Pearce raised his eyebrows in surprise. "It's for the fight back, of course."

"What? The hunger zombies?"

Pearce laughed. "Don't be silly, we've worked those out. The body-parts stop moving when you kill the brain, and yes, I suppose we can use the flamethrowers. You've seen what fire can do."

Jackson nodded and tried not to wince at the memory.

"No," Pearce continued, "this is all for the 'zillas. Until we get rid of them we can't start to rebuild."

Jackson looked at the weapons and the ragged assembly of survivors and the still-thinking undead. "We're going to use a load of powerful weapons to rebuild civilization?"

Pearce nodded. "Pretty much."

Jackson thought about it for a moment, and thought about the history of what had been the human race. "Fair enough," he said, and went to help the others unload.

Hair of the Dog

Apart from a few places with well-fuelled generators, or some other kind of backup that Brandon couldn't quite imagine, the power was out. And that meant that the Lincoln Tunnel had reached the state that he'd been so glad to avoid on his way out of the city.

"Is there no better way?" he asked Zach.

"The bridges are out," his friend replied. "It's this or another of the tunnels, and that would just mean more walking."

Brandon nodded. He'd known the answer before he even asked it, but he really didn't want to head into the darkness.

It had been Zach at the door of the video shop. He'd seen Brandon on the street and followed him back to the store. He'd then waited two days – so he related once he'd convinced Brandon to let him in – because he wasn't sure how his friend would cope with the fact that he was dead.

That wasn't what was bothering Brandon, it turned out. He'd now worked out the whole zombie thing – he'd had the time to observe them – and realised that those previously dead and then animated by the advent of the apocalypse were the traditional, ravening creatures. But those who had been killed by the events of the end of the world, and since, were just as they had been, if lacking a pulse and with a bit of a depthless hunger.

No, what was bothering Brandon was that Zach was all on his own.

He knew it was silly, that it was becoming an obsession, but the fact that Zach didn't know where Ashley was set him off into an angry rant.

"How can you not know? You were with her. You were with all of them? I was trampled to the ground and left to die – thank you very much for that, by the way, some friend you are! – but you were with her. Why couldn't you keep her with you? Why couldn't you keep her safe and bring her to me?"

Zach let him burn himself out, albeit with a *sotto voce*, "I did die, you know," and then suggested they return to the city to look for her.

"It's the most logical place. If she's alive, she'd want to stay near to home. And if she's dead, well, she'll be fine. Look at me!"

"What about the Godzilla things?" Brandon had asked.

Zach shrugged. "They're big, we're small. We can run and they can barely see us. It'll be fine. And they're not really like Godzilla, you know."

That had been that, and now they were walking through the darkened tunnel and back into New York.

Zach, with eyesight which he claimed had been enhanced by his demise, led the way. Brandon held onto the back of his shirt and pushed his feet in front of him, searching for obstacles. He was aware that if anyone could have seen him, with his outstretched arms and his shuffling, they would have thought he was the zombie, not Zach.

It seemed like hours, but it was still light when they emerged into the city.

And there they stopped as rockets launched from the backs of the two trucks parked on the approaches either side of the tunnel.

Brandon and Zach said nothing, just stared in shock, as the vapour trails traced their way deeper into the city and impacted with the head of a Godzilla, which exploded into red mist.

"Happy to be home?" Zach asked.

The 15th Incarnation

He had always known that he would be reincarnated. It had happened before, and it would happen again. He might find himself elsewhere in the world, and he might even be female this time. That was what he believed.

And now that he had died, he believed something else. He was not a woman, nor a foreigner. He was himself. Himself as he had been. He lacked a pulse, it was true, and for a time that had been distracted during meditation. But now he was glad for the peace, the stillness at his centre.

And he was glad for the second chance; the chance to do something truly special for what remained of the human race.

He sat cross-legged in the middle of the street. Guwahati was an empty shade. No traffic would disturb him. No crowds clamoured for him. He closed his eyes and reached once more for his centre and found it exactly where he knew it would be.

He nodded and smiled. All was ready.

When he opened his eyes again, he lifted his head and looked down the length of Lokhra Road. In front of him were stationary cars and burned and wrecked buildings.

And beyond those was a lizard which stretched up high enough to block the late morning sun.

He smiled at the monster, and reached out from his centre. He smiled, and he beckoned, and the ground shook under him as the monster approached.

When no more than two footsteps would have killed him outright, the creature stopped. It peered down at the small figure on the ground beneath it, and then it slowly dropped to one knee. And then to the other.

It rested back on its haunches, and lifted its head to the sky. A keening resonated all around, stirring insects into the air, and he reached out a hand in friendship.

Cull

DEFRA training didn't cover the ending of the world. When the fire started to rain from the sky Trevor had been in his car, making early morning visits to farms. He had taken shelter in a farmhouse while the buildings around were destroyed, and it had been his home since. He hadn't known what else to do.

The pantry had been well stocked with tinned and packet food, and the water had kept running, so that had been okay. And he had been able to hide behind the curtains and the sturdy front door, as people crossed the fields. He would have gone out and sought help, but some of them lurched in a way that worried Trevor, so he had stayed inside.

But this morning, through the light fog which had covered the land, he had seen a single figure who seemed to be walking normally, and so finally he had decided to venture forth.

"Hey!" He waved with both arms as he walked across the farmyard. The man in the field stopped and turned around in a circle before seeing the motion of Trevor's arms and changing his direction. As he drew closer, Trevor saw that the man was carrying a shotgun. He also saw that the man's skin was unnaturally pale, and that he had a raw wound in his shoulder. And finally, he saw that this was a man he recognised.

"You!" said the man, levelling the shotgun at Trevor, who instantly raised his arms again, but this time in surrender rather than welcome.

Trevor didn't know the man's name, but he knew his face. In all his recent badger-related visits to farms, this man had been present, protesting the cull.

"What the hell are you doing here?" the man asked.

Trevor really didn't know how to answer that question. And the wavering shotgun that was pointed at his chest wasn't helping him think.

He pointed with a crooked finger, his hands still above his head. "What happened to your shoulder?" he asked.

The man glanced down and the gun barrel dipped and then rose to stare Trevor in the face.

"I got bit. What does it look like?"

"Are you okay?"

"Course I'm not okay. I'm dead, aren't I?"

Trevor gaped, unsure if this was a joke or not. The man certainly looked dead, but he was also walking and talking.

Then the man raised the gun to his shoulder and pulled the trigger.

Trevor ducked his head in a wince and clapped his hands over his ears. He waited for the pain, but nothing came, so he opened his eyes again and looked down. He hadn't been hit.

When he looked up again he saw the smoking gun, but it was pointed away from him.

He looked to the side and saw a body lying on the ground.

Forgetting his antagonist for the moment, and letting his hands drop, he stepped towards the corpse. This body looked like it had been dead long before the shotgun blast had removed its head. Flesh had rotted from its limbs, and the suit it had been wearing was dirty and torn.

"What the hell?" he wondered aloud.

"I always said you knew nothing," said a voice at his side. "I don't know where you've been hiding, but the dead are walking the earth. There's the new ones, like me, who will hold a conversation and limit their hunger to crisps and cheese sandwiches – most of the time. And then there are those like our friend here who will strip the flesh from your bones as soon as look at you."

Trevor felt something knock against his hand and bit back a scream. He looked down and the man was pushing a long knife into his hand. "Into the eye," the man said. "It's hard, but you need to get the brain. That's how it works. And I'm keeping the gun."

Trevor nodded dumbly, as though any of this made sense.

"Now, come one. We have a cull to do. A proper one."

Worship

Todd had launched himself from his tent, sure he would die. The gang of looters had been shocked by his sudden appearance. They had still been human, still alive, and of the ten of them, two were women and one was a little boy. He had killed them all without sustaining a single wound.

When he was done, he stood amongst the bodies, their blood cooling on his skin, and tentatively praised the Lord for preserving him.

Without looking back at his refuge, he made his way from the shop with the knife still clutched in his hand.

The street was deserted, and Todd wandered down the centre of it. He wasn't worried that he might be exposed, that he might be attacked. He knew that he was protected.

And then, of course, on the next block, he saw a church. And the door was open. And singing was coming from inside.

Todd wandered in, still holding the knife down by his side.

Inside, it was dark, but full. The pews held rank upon rank of worshippers, holding their hands in the air and chanting: "All hail Shub-

Niggurath. All hail the Black Goat of the Woods with a Thousand Young. All hail Cthulhu who sleeps in R'lyeh. Hail! Hail! Hail!"

Todd didn't understand the words, yet found himself joining their chant. "All hail Yibb-Tstill. All hail Yog-Sothoth, the Dweller on the Threshold, outside of time and space yet kept within all. Hail! Hail! Hail!"

He walked down the aisle, feeling faces turning to face them, vaguely aware that they were lacking human features and there were more tentacles than there should have been. But he didn't care. The chant held him.

"All hail Nyarlathotep, the crawling chaos. All hail Hastur and Rlim Shiakorth, Nug and Yeb and Bugg-Shash. Hail! Hail! Hail!"

Todd did not notice as the walls and ceilings skewed themselves into non-Euclidian angles. He knelt at the altar without noticing the light coming through the windows in the nave, coating it in a strange colour, a colour from outer space.

A priest stepped forward. He wore a human face, and a dark robe. He placed his hand on Todd's head. He spoke, and even through the chanting Todd heard him.

"Welcome, my son. My name is Father Pickman. You are now in the right place. This world is now the right world. We are ready. The old ones are come. Welcome."

Todd sighed, and finally he felt the rapture lift him.

Orders

"Sir, we have established a link," came the voice over the intercom. General Xorle-Jian-Splein levered himself up in his bed, and leant on one of his elbows to face the microphone.

"It's about kzplecking time!" he bellowed. "Do you need me now?"

"Whenever you are ready, sir, it is a stable connection and they are willing to talk."

"Good," the general said, and slapped the off button as he slumped backwards onto his bunk.

He had spent most of the last weeks in his bed. Orders from Xulxaxia had been that he should wait and see what happened, but after the anticipation of the attack, the waiting had sent him into a deep depression.

Now, maybe, finally, he would have something to do, he just needed to find some energy so he could do it.

After a moment gathering himself, he pushed his bulk up and out of bed, then slouched his way to the bridge.

When he got there, the lizard working at communications was waiting expectantly. A crackling was emerging from the speaker in the panel in front of him.

"Standby," the lizard said, as the general approached.

"Confirmed," came a deep growl of a voice, then the screen in the panel cleared and General Xorle-Jian-Splein was greeted by a saurian face which was composed of scales and teeth, with two deep-set red eyes.

The face reminded the general of his mother.

"General Zorl?" the voice asked.

In deference either to the lizard he was talking to, or to the memory of his dear departed Mammy, Xorle-Jian-Splein nodded without adding a correction.

"We have the planet. It is ours. Leave."

Deference fled. "You fucking what!? Who the fuck do you think you are?"

The Saurian smiled. "I think I am the Grand Admiral Xunthian-Splenshun-Cthulhu-Homite, leader of the Black Fleet, sent here several thousand years ago to wait. I have waited long enough. Our time is now. We have the planet. You are no longer needed."

Xorle-Jian-Splein reeled. The Black Fleet? Xunthian-Splenshun-Cthulhu-Homite? He was a legend, truly a legend. Xorle-Jian-Splein had been told stories of him when he was growing up. He had believed that the man was a myth, but here he was, talking to him.

"But… but… sir!" the general protested.

"But, nothing. You have your orders. We are

active, we are in control. You are no longer useful. Out." And the screen went black.

General Xorle-Jian-Splein stood and stared. He had seen the footage of the huge figures bestriding the planet beneath, but he had had no idea that he was watching the martial tactics of creatures so impressive they were all but Gods to his race.

"What are our orders, sir?" asked the pilot.

"We... we..."

"Sir?"

The general's voice was almost a whisper as he issued his order. "We go home," he said, and then turned and slumped his way back to his bunk.

The Beginning

A butterfly flapped its wings...

...and a tree fell, catching on a power line and ripping it to the ground; because the tree was hit by a stampeding elephant; because the elephant had been startled by a monkey jumping from a tree; because a fallen petal had caused the monkey to sneeze; because the wingbeats of the butterfly had caused the petal to fall.

A butterfly flapped its wings...

...and a boy typed a piece of code which he sent out into the internet; because he had discovered a loophole in a firewall which hadn't been there before; because a server had blown out in a buried computer room; because a workload had been rerouted through the server; because a section of the network had stopped operating; because a tree fell, catching on a power line and ripping it to the ground.

A butterfly flapped its wings...

...and in one small place for one brief time, the universe tore in two; because the particles in the supercollider were too dense and travelling too fast; because the information had been corrupted in the computers; because a virus had infected them; because a boy typed a piece of code which he sent out into the internet.

A butterfly flapped its wings…

… and fire rained down from the skies; and zombies and giant alien lizards walked the earth; and the human race died and disappeared in their millions; because what could and couldn't be collided; because the possibilities of time and space all existed in a single moment; because in one small place and for one brief time, the universe tore in two; because a butterfly flapped its wings.

The Final Party

The crashing rumble of the fall of the headless lizard reached them and a cheer went up. Brandon and Zach looked around, still surprised by the welcoming party they had stumbled upon.

A closer look showed Brandon that the assembled group was not the contingent of soldiers that he had presumed, but was instead a ragged bunch made up from, yes, some soldiers, but mostly civilians. Some were men, some women, some little more children; some of them were dead.

In response to their success they were exchanging high-fives and hugs. And then a voice shouted, "Brandon?" and he turned to see Ashley running towards him.

He stood and stared, unable to believe that he had finally found her. She ran up to him and he thought she was going to stop, but she didn't, and he was nearly knocked from his feet as she threw her arms around him.

He hugged her back, and then when she released him, he returned her kiss with passion.

Finally, she broke free, and grinned at him.

"I thought you were dead," she said.

"You too," he said, and was aware that he was also grinning.

Somehow, he had expected to find that she was a zombie. He had reconciled himself to the fact, and even tried to imagine what their relationship might be like. But although she looked dishevelled, and a little thinner, she was pink and healthy and alive.

He was about to say something more, when a gasp arose from the crowd.

Taking his hand in hers, she turned so they could see what everyone was looking at.

The monster that they had thought they'd killed with the rockets was once more standing. Its head was reforming, and it seemed larger and more fang-filled than before.

It turned to face the group who had attacked it, clearly focussing on them despite the distance. And then with a flex of its shoulders, huge wings opened on its back.

Brandon watched it, a feeling of awe turning to something like reverence in his chest. And then he heard words bubbling up from inside his chest; words which were echoed by all those around him.

"Hail!" they called. "Hail! Hail! Hail!"

Afterword

This collection of stories was written in January 2014, but it has a much longer pedigree.

In January 2011, I wrote 31 flash-fictions—one a day for the whole month—and they became my first self-published collection, *31*.

Then, from May in the same year, I started a project called *flash365*, and proceeded to write a flash-fiction a day for a whole year and post them to a blog. Each month of that year had a different theme, but one of them was to write a whole month of linked stories. That 'flash-fiction novella' was published by Salt in 2012 as *Braking Distance*.

Now, in 2014, I have decided to combine some of those earlier efforts. So, once again, I plan to write 365 stories within a single year. However, rather than one a day, I am writing a full collection per month, and self-publishing it. Each collection will contain the number of stories relative to the number of days in that month, hence the 31 stories in *Apocalypse*. This is the first of the collections, and if all goes to plan, it will be followed by 11 more. Some, like this one, will consist entirely of stories set around an event.

Some will be linked by a theme, or a character, or in some other way. The challenge is to make them complete books, not just gatherings of disparate stories, and I will be investigating the various ways in which that can happen.

If you have enjoyed this book, I hope you will look out for the others in the 2014 series. And if, after 2014 is over, there aren't quite 12 of them, I hope you will forgive me!

Happy reading and, don't worry, it really isn't the end of the world.

Yet.

Calum Kerr
Southampton
27-01-14

Other books from **Gumbo Press**:

www.gumbopress.co.uk

Enough by Valerie O'Riordan

Fake mermaids and conjoined twins, Johannes Gutenberg, airplane sex, anti-terrorism agricultural advice, Bluebeard and more.

Ten flash-fictions.

Threshold by David Hartley

Threshold explores the surreal and the strange through thirteen flash-fictions which take us from a neighbour's garden, out into space, and even as far as Preston. But which Preston?

Undead at Heart by Calum Kerr

War of the Worlds meets *The Walking Dead* in this novel from Calum Kerr, author of *31* and *Braking Distance*

Made in the USA
Lexington, KY
02 May 2014